"Hi, Pizza Man!"

by VIRGINIA WALTER

pictures by PONDER GOEMBEL

Purple House Press   Kentucky

"Mama!"

"I know you're hungry, Vivian.
It's so hard to wait
for the pizza man to come.
He'll be here soon."

"What will you say when the doorbell rings and we open the door?"

"What if it's not a pizza man?
What if it's a pizza woman?
Then what will you say?"

"Hi, Pizza Woman!"

"What if it's not a pizza woman? What if it's a pizza kitty?
Then what will you say?"

"MEOW MEOW, PIZZA KITTY!"

"What if it's a pizza dog? Then what will you say?"

"WOOF WOOF, PIZZA DOG!"

"What if it's a pizza duck? Then what will you say?"

"QUACK QUACK, PIZZA DUCK!"

"What if it's a pizza cow? Then what will you say?"

"MOOO O O O, PIZZA COW!"

"What if it's a pizza snake? Then what will you say?"

SSSSSSSS, PIZZA SNAKE!"

"What if it's a pizza dinosaur? Then what will you say?"

"ROAR, PIZZA DINOSAUR!"

RING! RING!

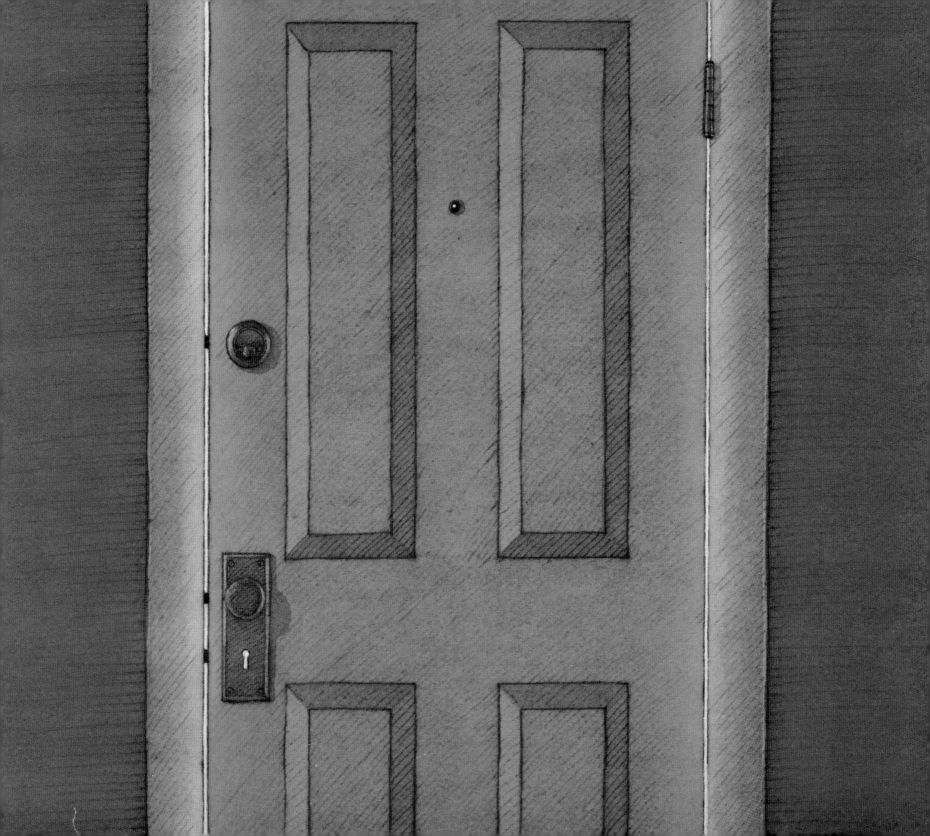

"Hi, Pizza MAN!"

For the Mitnick kid,
who is all grown up now.

—V.W.

To my grown-up Emma.

—P.G.

Published by Purple House Press, PO Box 787, Cynthiana, Kentucky 41031
Find more Classic Books for Kids at purplehousepress.com

Publisher's Cataloging-in-Publication
Walter, Virginia. "Hi, pizza man!" / by Virginia Walter; pictures by Ponder Goembel. p. cm.
Summary: While a young girl waits for the delivery of a hot pizza, she provides the appropriate animal sounds for a
variety of pretend animal pizza deliverers.
ISBN 13: 978-1-930900-94-3 (alk. paper)
[1. Animals sounds—Fiction.] I. Gombel, Ponder, ill. II. Title.
PZ7.W17126Hi 2017 [E]—dc21 2017937204

Printed in South Korea by PACOM
1 2 3 4 5 6 7 8 9 10
First Edition